Purchased with
Library Measure
Thank You Marin County voters!

S0-AXI-769

Marin Co. New Books
Fiction Widmer
The blue soda siphon :
31111035843836

1- 15

DATE DUE

FEB 1 8 2015	
MAR 2 8 2015	
⅟ 12/05	

PRINTED IN U.S.A.

The Blue Soda Siphon

THE SWISS LIST

The Blue Soda Siphon

URS WIDMER

Translated by Donal McLaughlin

LONDON NEW YORK CALCUTTA

Seagull Books, 2014

First published in 1992 as *Der blaue Siphon* by Urs Widmer
© Diogenes Verlag AG Zurich, 1992. All rights reserved.

First published in English translation by Seagull Books
English translation © Donal McLaughlin, 2014

ISBN   978 0 8574 2 211 8

British Library Cataloguing-in-Publication Data
A catalogue record for this book is available from the British
Library

Typeset in Cochin by Seagull Books, Calcutta, India
Printed and bound by Maple Press, York, Pennsylvania, USA

A few days ago, barely more than a week ago, I had a dream—a teeming crowd, some shouting, and suddenly I was in a hazy void, in space perhaps, and in front of me, as if raised on an invisible altar, floated a bottle, a soda siphon made of blue glass, gleaming in an otherwise invisible light that made it sparkle. Rainbow-colour flashes in the deep blue. I stared at this marvel and upon waking the next morning, thought for a while, confused, about the message, then forgot about it. Focused on everyday life again. Oil fields were burning. Bombs were falling on cities. Missiles were flying along avenues at the height of the traffic lights and detonating when they reached the end. People had stared at the sky like this before, in Dresden, in Coventry, and had seen the planes, then the black dots falling towards them, and the women covered their children's ears before they were blown to pieces. Others, running off, slower than the poisons in the air, then had writhed like this in the streets. In Pompeii, people had run, too late, to the harbour like this, the burning rain was faster. Napalm storms tore through shanty villages like this. Hordes of Huns slew peasant like this as their legs scrambled into haystacks. The Russians perished in a burning Moscow like this. The shoeless French too, in the snow, the Berezina still far in the distance. Unloved, Napoleon bit the dust like this. Feeling no emotion, the Vietnamese killed millions of Cambodians like this or the Cambodians millions of Vietnamese — who remembers now? The Jews. The victors, alive still, endure their victories and the dead are dead. Who can actually name a victim? Oil fields were burning, at any rate, and everyday life consisted of me asking my daughter about her homework and not forgetting to order the mineral water. And listening to the news, hourly.

In the evening that day, a Friday, I went to the cinema, a city-centre cinema showing a film of which I knew only the name and that it had been praised in the morning paper or evening news. I'd confused it with something else, presumably, as the film was peculiar—more than just odd—not my taste. I was also completely alone in the cinema. Maybe it *was* a Monday. As ever I sat at the front, in the very first row, as I like to drown in films. Those widescreen films are already a thing of the past now, those CinemaScope worlds I could plunge into so deeply, I could never see everything, only parts, like in real life. For example, only when I saw *Doctor Zhivago* on TV much later—a moveable postage stamp, in comparison—did I realize that I'd seen but part of the action, on the right of the screen or the left. That Julie Christie was at one point completely naked in the doorway, for example, had escaped me. I could recall only the doctor's blank gaze. So there I was, in the front row again. That I was alone I noticed only on the way out. There may have been a great many people in at the beginning but the film had driven them out. I had stayed. I don't know why. Probably because where I come from, you savour every last bite you've paid for.

The film was black and white, no blue at all, and I'd struggle to say what actually happened in it. It was old, in any case, silent maybe, made in the twenties or thirties and set in India or Pakistan or Bangladesh. Who can tell those far-off lands apart? Calcutta or Hecuba — the men wore turbans and were naked to the waist and the women were wrapped in sarees. Had dots on their brows. The film was about a fortune-teller who lived high on the roof of a house, surrounded by chickens and goats that grazed on the concrete roof. He was as old as the hills, maybe even a woman — sporting not a beard but scarves that could, however, have also concealed a beard. Children, his grandchildren perhaps, dragged passers-by up to him. They didn't use force, rather, whispered promises, allured the people with their deep gazes and so,

again and again, women unhappy in love and
nearly bankrupt merchant princes climbed the
stairs, never-ending labyrinths from which no man
or woman would ever find their way back down
without the children's help. If you refused to pay,
you weren't led out, you would instead spend
hours, days, in a labyrinthine hell, passing through
kitchens and tailors' workshops and dormitories
full of mattresses without ever returning to solid
ground. From time to time, a child would cross
your path and look at you inquiringly and, in the
end, even the most stubborn would concede defeat
and drop all their rupees into that outstretched
hand. He, or she, was expensive, this fortune-teller.
Often dozens would be seeking help, sitting among
the goats and chickens, waiting to be admitted
to the shack. Rich men, maharajas maybe, seemed
to sit just as patiently as ancient beggars for
whom it was hard to imagine a future. Right at
the beginning, a young man in a tropical suit —
including the helmet — was enticed into the hallway
by a barefoot boy. He hesitated, wanted to go back,
back to his wife, a teenage girl beneath a pink

parasol surrounded by the bustle of the street, her hand out, pleading, but it was too late already, already he was climbing the stairs, determined to complete the adventure — 'Wait for me!' he called back in English into the sunlight — and when he reached the top he was the only customer and the young guide left him with a woman — she too almost a child still — peeking out through the curtains of the shack and waving to him. His down-less face dripped with sweat. Inside the shack a terrible heat. The fortune-teller, the man or woman, barely visible in the poor light. He or she looked for a long time, then foretold the truth. The young European though, British surely, had eyes only for the woman — who had lowered her eyes and was crouching beside the old man, her father or, perhaps, more probably, her grandmother — and so didn't understand what he'd been told. He stood up and paid and laughed though for no reason. The woman, who had understood perfectly well, began to lead him back down, then stopped on a step and turned and burrowed her lips into his, which was how his wife discovered them both. She'd ventured into the labyrinth alone, then screamed and moaned and fainted, and came to again to find her husband patting her cheeks. Eventually, both were ready to be led out. A final kiss from the woman, for the wife too, whose eyes though were Fury-like, mortally wounded. Then the two walked off towards the destiny awaiting them at the end of the street, fatal in the case of the wife — a fanatic who hated everything British shot her — whereas the man, for as long as he lived, was never to leave the town, instead he searched and searched in vain for the woman he'd seen in the labyrinth of those stairs.

I staggered out of the cinema into the night. It was dark now. Much warmer than two hours earlier. Wind was rustling in the trees. I went up Rämistrasse, lost in thought, unable to forget the film. I knew neither the name of the director nor that of the actress. The closing credits had been in a foreign script. I crossed Heimplatz where at that moment there were no trams or cars. The street lights were faulty or at least the lamps weren't on. In Hottingerstrasse, a vehicle did then turn up, a noisy vintage car with blue headlights, the first noise in this otherwise silent night. The driver invisible. It made me jump though I didn't know why and I began to walk faster. Rushed across the square full of trees and bushes close to where I lived, *live*, and was soon standing outside my house that no longer had a bell but a new door. I pounded on it, calling, 'Isabelle! What's all this?' and finally a head became visible on the first floor, not of Isabelle but of a man shouting he was going to call the police. I said I lived here, asked what *he* was doing here, who he was, and when he slammed the window shut and didn't budge, and when Isabelle didn't answer either, *I* went to the police.

Bent over a typewriter was an officer who had obviously been sleeping. He looked at me, blinking. He was wearing a hussar-style uniform, like at festival time, and now put on a belt with a huge pistol and came shuffling over to the barrier where I was standing. His dull eyes looked at me and suddenly I was no longer able to confess to him that Isabelle was lying beneath a strange man, in a house without a bell and with the wrong door, so I muttered something confused about the street lights being off and the officer said he knew nothing about a blackout. ID card? I didn't have one, pretended not to have heard and left, ran when he shouted, 'Stop!' and, as I huddled behind a bush and he came tearing down the front steps, even, 'Or I'll shoot!' I held my breath as he stood right before me, baffled, looking up and down Hottingerstrasse. Finally, he disappeared into the station again. Something had been odd, about the fittings, that barrier was new and the telephone, an ancient monstrosity of black Bakelite, hadn't been there on my last visit either. I'd visited the station barely two weeks before, after all, to pay a parking fine I'd found beneath the wiper of my car, parked in the blue zone, despite the fact that I'd jammed my residents' parking permit in behind the steering wheel. The 'Police' sign outside was new too, with letters reminiscent of films from the Nazi period.

I then loitered around the house for a few hours after all. It stood there, deathly quiet and black. Who was the man? Someone from that group that Isabelle occasionally set off for, to discuss human affectivity in the late twentieth century? Finally, I abandoned my home and wandered aimlessly around the town, in the light of early morning, watery eyed, treating the avenue trees to kicks, cursing, until I reached the station and stumbled onto a train with the name of my home town on the front, Basel, and fell asleep on a wooden bench. I woke up because a ticket collector was shaking me, who, when I said, as coolly as possible given all that had happened to me, 'A single to Basel, with a rail card,' grabbed me by the collar and, cursing, threw me off. Fortunately, the train had stopped at the time, at the station in Muttenz, at a platform on which only a luggage trolley stood and, away up at the front, a soldier with a huge fur knapsack. I was too stunned to feel anything—the train set off again, hissing and squeaking—and so I left the station to complete the journey on foot. Basel isn't far from Muttenz and in his day Robert Walser walked from Zurich to Würzburg without stopping. The sun was shining. I was no longer crying. I wanted to face my situation head-on, not to return to Isabelle somehow for something like ten years or to kill the lover or batter her like no man has ever battered a woman until, black and blue and covered in red welts, she tearfully confessed the man's name to me.

And so I continued on a dirt track towards the town, towards that blue hill which conceals the rest of the country from it and at which the needle of my compass had pointed from the very beginning, at a tower on it, to be precise, the town's water tower that was now turning up on the horizon and which I'd often climbed. I'd never found out where the water promised by the name of the building could be. On the inside, you see, with the exception of a steep staircase, it was hollow and empty. My feet were hurting. Five or six helmeted soldiers cycled past with carbines on their backs, and, long after they'd passed, the last one turned and came back and asked something I didn't understand. Where I was. He was sweating, seemed agitated, wore rimless glasses beneath his steel helmet and, though he'd cycled at quite a speed, had a cigarette in his mouth. When I answered, though, in the language of my home region, of my childhood—that I was here, and walking because I was in no hurry to reach my destination—he let up on me, mumbled something that, again, I didn't understand and cycled on. On the rear mudguard of his bicycle—a private ladies' bicycle, whereas his comrades were on those army models that can withstand a nuclear strike—the number plate was rattling, a badly attached red plate. 'BL 41,' it read. I lingered for a while, motionless, watching the soldier get smaller as he chased after his comrades. Finally, I understood. The shock, perhaps joy, paralysed me so much that I sat down. I sank into flowers. Forget-me-nots, poppies, daisies. Clover. Behind me, a forest smelling of damp leaves. A deep peace lay over the country. The buzzing of bees and bumblebees was the loudest thing you could hear. In front of me a wide, green plain—the Rhine Plain—over which the blue sky arched. I took deep breaths in a way I hadn't done for a long time, stretched out my arms and sighed and groaned and laughed and shook my head.

When I reached the water tower, I could no longer feel my feet or felt them in a way that suggested they couldn't be mine. I was no longer used to walking and was wearing shoes I'd bought on a holiday in Portugal, meant for the short distances between the beach, bungalow and pizza bar. I didn't yet want to go—where? *home*? was that the right word? Not immediately. Didn't want to go to that house that stood a few hundred metres away, exactly as I remembered it, to that white Bauhaus cube I'd not seen for an absolute eternity. A young architect, uncompromisingly progressive, had built it, with a flat roof and curtain-less windows that went right down to the ground, all the way round, so that not a single corner remained for anything secret. He'd later moved to the GDR, after the war that was raging now, and had been given a professorship and two Stalin Prizes and not a single commission. Embittered, he'd returned to the bitter West and died in a house that had crooked walls since it had been built, without an architect, by a master builder of the old school.

At the top, I stood on the panorama terrace that ran round the round tower. I was a little dizzy. I've always had difficulty with towers, with the sheer height of towers, as if something could happen to me that I know nothing about. The leaning tower in Pisa, I'd also preferred to admire from below. At the top of the Empire State Building, I'd been glad of the barbed-wire defences and also of a girlfriend who clung to me. Here, I stood bent over the railing, looking out across the country. The distant town, with the cathedral towers and the glistening Rhine that, away in the background, disappeared into the mist of enemy territory. Below, mothers and nannies were laughing. Crops were rippling, birds were flying, a butterfly right in front of me, so high above the flowers! That house, the white cube, lay quietly in the sunlight. The windows were reflecting. The huge aerial that would later be felled by lightning and crash into the garden—I was being battered by my friend Hans Arm at the time and was saved by the bang—still loomed into the sky from the flat roof. The garden was full of potato plants. The birches that would later shroud the house were still dwarf-sized. I didn't let it out of my sight. None of it. Just once, a dog ran out into the garden and vanished, as if on an invisible rubber leash, straight back in through an invisible door.

I went to the porthole near where the staircase ended and that was as narrow and low as in an old cathedral. You had to stoop and when I lowered my head to take my first step back down, a woman, gasping from the steep climb and white in the face, white as chalk in the face, was blocking my way. She walked past me without seeing me or looking at me, though we'd almost—accidentally—kissed, and stood at the railings round the terrace. She hung herself over them like a piece of clothing put out to dry. Her arms, even her head, hung out in the air and, occasionally, her feet in blue-leather sandals lifted off the ground. She said something though she was alone. It sounded quiet though she'd perhaps shouted. I joined her, addressing her back, 'What were you talking about just now?'

She slumped back onto her feet, straightened up and turned to me. She was wearing round glasses and the lenses had misted over. The dull glass was concealing her eyes.

'About love, if I'm not mistaken?'

'You are mistaken,' she muttered. 'And you're not mistaken.'

15

She took her glasses off and wiped them clean, examining me with her short-sighted eyes. She was young, her hair as short and her expression as fierce as Joan of Arc's when still buoyed by her virginity. 'I said I was made for love. But I didn't say it to you.'

'But to?'

'To no one. To the air. No one is made for my love. Every man I meet seems to be coated with ice. Or am I? How can we get us to melt?'

'I guess I can't help you with that,' I said.

'No.'

She put her glasses back on. The lenses were immediately dull again. She shrugged her shoulders and with a wave of her hand pointed at all that lay before her. It was as if she were spreading her wings, a wing. 'Isn't that beautiful? Isn't this country magnificent?'

'I haven't seen anything as beautiful for a very very long time,' I said.

'Farewell,' she said, turning away and adopting her original position. I hesitated but I'd been forgotten. She was speaking to birds again, or angels.

I ran down the stairs, landed on the hot gravel. Children had marked out a hopscotch grid with their shoes and were hopping and jumping.   A young woman, who didn't seem to have a child with her, was sitting on a wall, looking at me. How did I know none of this happy gang was hers? She was almost a girl herself, chinless, with red hair and breasts that were threatening to make the buttons on her child's blouse pop. She was a little fat and smiled at me. I blushed, or hopped and jumped, delighted, but I had no time to lose, of course, and swiftly walked along a path, as straight as a die, towards an old fort, a fortification from earlier times, now overgrown with bushes. My ears dragged behind, eagerly pricked up for any conversation taking place behind me. I was breathing loudly. The gravel crunched beneath my feet. As I walked along the wall, smelling the odours from the many portholes—mildew, dung, animals—I thought I heard something like a scream. But it could also have been the cheer of a child playing hide-and-seek who, eyes closed and huddled behind a bin, had just been found by his mama. The fortification, incidentally, was not very old, one hundred and sixty years, or — if I counted back from my reclaimed lifetime — one hundred and ten. The men of the canton of Basel Land had fought a battle against those from Basel Stadt and liberated themselves from their arrogance. Ever since, plates with BL on them rattle on bicycles if the cyclist is from Basel Land and with BS if the cyclist is from the town itself. Taking the bend round the fort, I looked back briefly at the tower. People were running to and fro. Some were standing still. That was as much as I was able, and wished, to make out.

The house, the cube, was stand-offish from close up too. It invited me in nonetheless. I hesitated, a bit perplexed, at the garden gate, its handle warm in my hand. Above me, in a tree originally from Japan, probably, were tiny little red apples that tasted horrible, even now when I bit into one. So sour, your mouth formed a tiny *o*. The granite slabs that led up to the front door were glistening in the sun, hot when I touched them with one hand. Finally, I had reason to take off my shoes, my socks.

I put both beneath a bush with little blue berries. Then stood, groaning, on the stone path. Blind, my arms hugging me, listening only to my burning soles. I then went up to the front door and opened it. A staircase, carpeted, the carpet held in place by brass rods. I climbed the few steps and pushed the door to the flat open. 'Hello? Anyone home?'

The dog shot out of the kitchen, raced yelping towards me and, licking me enthusiastically, jumped at me. Hardly able to fend him off, I laughed and tried to save my face from his tongue. My mother appeared with a kitchen knife in her hand. She was wearing a bright summer dress and had a dish towel tucked into a narrow leather belt. She looked at us, the amorous dog and me, fighting back and giggling, and shouted, 'Jimmy! heel!' And to me, 'Couldn't you have rung the doorbell?'

'I didn't see a doorbell,' I said, pushing the dog away. 'I never ring of late. I've no luck with doorbells.'

'And why aren't you wearing shoes?'

'I've no luck with shoes either,' I said, and had to laugh as I thought, I don't have a quick tongue any more. That surprises you, eh? 'I was thinking, you could perhaps offer me some work, in the garden, or something.'

She was now holding the dog by the collar. It was standing on its hind legs, panting and trying to get to me. She was younger than me, much younger, a severe beauty with a Roman nose and black hair hanging well down her back. She was holding the knife like a weapon, at chest level, whereas the dog, a little terrier, seemed to be more on my side. Through a half-open door, the one to the living room, some light fell onto the floor, a streak of sunshine refracted through glass somewhere — a colour bar, a whole rainbow, was flowing across my feet. I wanted to glance into the room — could see something too, a round coffee table and two or three armchairs — but my mother was faster and closed the door. The blade of the kitchen knife now pointed at me and her eyes had a frightened look.

'I won't do you any harm,' I said. 'I've never done anything to you. Do you have children?'

'One,' she said, sounding a little sharp. 'He's . . .'

'Stop it, you daft brute!' I shouted, almost simultaneously. The dog had broken free and was licking my feet like a madman.

'Does the dog know you?' My mother seemed to be thrown by what was happening, her lips twitching, her eyes watery. She was speaking too loud. 'Just go over to the potatoes then! They're full of beetles. There's a bucket in the shed.'

I was already on the steps outside when I heard her speak again. 'Wait!' She appeared in the doorway and handed me a pair of heavy black shoes. I sat down on the top step and put them on. My father's shoes. They were too small for me. When I stood up to attempt my first few steps in them, the front door opened and the woman with the red hair and child's blouse I'd seen at the water tower rushed past, calling 'Madame! Madame!', and disappeared into the flat where, in frantic French, she spouted a story of which I understood

only the word tower and *femme*. That sufficed. I'd
known about the tragedy even as a child. No one
had been able to save the woman, the unfortunate
woman, not with kind words, nor by using force.
She smashed to the ground, on the gravel. My
mother remained inaudible. Her fate was different.
Over eighty in age, she physically assaulted a tram,
thinking she had priority, the right to cross first —
to no avail. As I hobbled to the front door, the
young woman came racing out of the flat and ran
upstairs, her red hair wafting behind her, and her
name came back to me. Lisette. I'd often been at the
tower with her, in the forest, in the garden. Where
might I be now?

Next, I was crouching, barefoot again, in the
potatoes that stretched far before me, as far as a
huge walnut tree. Thousands of beetles were indeed
on the leaves — tiny, pretty little creatures with
brown stripes on their yellow shells. I threw them
into the bucket and thought of my father and how,
in the old days, *so now*, he'd walked on the road,
hopping, as if he were a figure on the board of an
invisible Chinese chequers player, of some kind of

Orion, until I finally grasped that with each step he wanted to kill one of these beetles that were crawling everywhere. If, at any point, none were within reach, he froze on one leg, with a desperate look in his eyes, as if stepping on nothing would be fatal. I was still locked in these thoughts when my father indeed came hopping up the slabbed path, exactly the way I remembered, in uniform, with his glasses and cigarette. He was the cyclist at Muttenz. I hadn't recognized him. I hadn't recognized my own father! He wasn't wearing a steel helmet now, though. It was hanging from the handlebar of the ladies' bicycle that was leaning against the trunk of the Japanese apple tree. My father disappeared, like a jumping flea. He still had hair! I bent over the beetles again. By sunset, I was down at the walnut and the bucket was full.

I stood up. My back was sore. As if he'd been waiting for this moment, my father stepped out into the garden and came towards me. He was wearing flannels, a cardigan, and now looked much more familiar to me. He was smoking, of course. He looked like Gustav Mahler when he had yet to achieve anything, or like Jean-Paul Sartre before he left school. 'Don't overdo it!' he said, holding his right hand out to me. 'Herr — ?'

I told him my name.

'You don't say!' He looked at me, sceptically, from below as he was smaller than me. 'From the Aargau branch of the family or the Thurgau?'

'My father is from Wyna Valley,' I said. I held the bucket out to him. The first beetles were trying to escape over the rim.

'Mine too,' he said, taking the bucket. 'Me too. We must be related, actually.'

'I am your son,' I said.

'Listen, any other time, yes. But I'm not in the mood for jokes today.' I knew how much he liked to laugh. Something, indeed, seemed to be occupying him — nothing to do with me. 'Besides, you look more like my father. But you're not him. I know my father.'

'And your son?'

He looked at me — furious? frightened? — took the bucket and walked towards the house. He was

still in good health! 'You shouldn't smoke so much!'
I called after him. 'It will kill you!' He stopped, not
in response to my warning but because of a piece of
paper that he lifted, then put down in the grass.
When I reached the spot, it turned out to be a
crumpled five-franc note. I put it in my pocket
though it didn't look particularly valid any more and
watched my father disappear into the house with the
bucket. Did he want to put it in the kitchen for his
wife? I'd have liked to talk to him about something
that interested him and about which I also knew
now, Villon's ballads or Diderot's work on the
Encyclopédie, or the nun from Portugal who didn't go
to the toilet for forty years and then shat stones. He
loved all these books. I could also have told him that
I'd met a man whose ambition was to rewrite the
oeuvre of Henry Miller, to write a new version. He'd
chosen Miller because he didn't know a single line
of his work and because the titles sounded so good.
Now, in chronological order, he was writing new
texts to fit those titles, his own texts, texts that fit.
In his *Tropic of Cancer*, for example, he covered the
fate of a whole family, every member of which fell

ill with the same kind of cancer and, made more aware by their suffering, each died happier than all those who are well. At the moment — in my time and his, I mean — he was working on *The Colossus of Maroussi*, in his case set in deepest Africa, as the Maroussi for him were a belligerent tribe somewhere in Mali who wanted to give it to the whites once and for all. My father would have liked that kind of story, I knew, leaving aside the fact that he couldn't be familiar with *The Colossus of Maroussi*, given that Miller, no doubt, at this very moment, was working on the final chapter in his quiet cave in Clichy. — Probably, I'd have liked above all to tell him that he'd just died when I'd written a book and then another and another.

I walked along the house towards the garden gate. Music droned through the closed windows, brassy Mozart, and behind the curtainless aquarium vitrines stood my father and my mother, talking intensely — inaudibly, as the music was louder. I fetched my shoes and socks from beneath the bush, put them on, took the bicycle — the helmet I hung on a branch of the tree — jumped onto the saddle and rode off. How often I'd ridden this bicycle! It was my bicycle, actually. My parents had bought it—and its male equivalent—when the Nazis were approaching and they had to fear having to flee in a mad rush. It weighed a ton, was black, a British make called Strand, and though I try out every kind of bicycle to this day, I've never seen another Strand. My parents must have bought up every single one. On the bicycle which I was now pedalling through the crop fields, with no hands and singing like a good-for-nothing, I'd zoomed into town, for instance, when it was bombed near the end of the war, and had stood wide-eyed near the smoking houses on Tellstrasse. On another occasion, a whole Motul oil tank had exploded in the Dreispitz district and again my bicycle had taken me to the scene of the disaster.

It was dark and I pressed the dynamo against the tyre of the front wheel. It sang as expected. But the pedalling had become laborious, also because I was heading towards the Jura Mountains. I noticed I was tired, downright exhausted—the previous night, after all, fifty years ago, I'd not

slept or only that little bit on the slow train to
Muttenz. I went into an inn, its windows had a
friendly glow. Soldiers at every table. Incredibly
thick smoke. I considered what I could afford and
ordered a cervelat with bread and a beer. Mustard
would surely be free. A harsh Valkyrie served me.
She was wearing some kind of traditional costume
and had those blond braids looped round her head
that were also popular in the North. The soldiers
were making a racket though posters on the wall
said that the enemy was listening. I ate with a
ravenous appetite. Then I waved to the Valkyrie
and asked if she had a spare bed anywhere.

'You're in luck,' she said. 'The landlord's son is
away today. You can have his.'

'And what does it cost?'

'The cervelat is one-fifty, the beer, forty. So,
one-ninety, right? Plus the room, five. Six-ninety,
in total.'

'I've only five francs,' I said.

She looked at me and shrugged. Put the empty
glasses on the table onto a large metal tray and
began to forget me. I took my wallet out.

'Wait!' I called. 'Look!' I took a note out. 'You're still young. If you wait forty years — less, even — that will be worth twenty francs.'

She took the note, looked at it, held it against the light of the lamp and laughed. 'What's that supposed to be?'

'Money.' I laughed too. 'It's not valid yet. It's a matter of being patient.'

'Do you make them yourself?' She gave my note to one of the soldiers, who also marvelled at it, laughed and gave it to his neighbour. It made its way round the whole inn. They all thought the joke was great. My neighbour, a Fusilier with a red, almost blue, face thumped me on the shoulder, excitedly. 'A beer for the old gentleman!' he called and the Valkyrie brought it over to me, and then a few more. And when it was closing time, she said quietly just to creep into the the landlord's son's room, for heaven's sake, the first room on the first floor, and for free. Not until the next day when I was cycling in the warm morning sun between the firs of Freiberge did I ask myself where the twenty-franc note had ended up and with whom.

It was about noon when I emerged from the
dark forest and stood on a hill above the village
Isabelle comes from. It lay in a hollow between
green meadows full of flowers, amid the bluster of
millions of bees. Birds were chasing one another.
The church bell sounded. A cock crowed, belatedly,
and dogs were barking. In a narrow field, a farmer
was walking. Was he still sowing seeds? So late?
But there were still patches of snow at the edges of
the forest, the village lay high up, closer to God,
closer to the cold. I walked, pushing the bicycle
down a narrow footpath, and was soon among
houses, among gardens where chickens were
scrabbling and bedsheets were drying on long
wires. No children anywhere, no people, only at the
entrance of a barn two old men standing with
pitchforks. I strolled here and there, crossed the
village square several times, a fountain was gurgling
at its centre. I went round the church and even over
the small cemetery where I found Isabelle's name
too, not hers of course, that of some great-great-
aunt or other. From an unremarkable house came
the sudden screaming of children. I'd found the

school. My heart did flutter, it's true, but Isabelle couldn't possibly be at this school, she was only two, would go to this school only in a few years' time, to be taught by a Mademoiselle Gass she'd often told me about, as Mademoiselle Gass, an inconsolable spinster who was never to be consoled, tyrannized her pupils, including Isabelle, whose hair she once pulled out, until, one day, she just wasn't there any more. Isabelle later learnt that her teacher had spent the remainder of her days in the lunatic asylum at Epalinges.

Suddenly, I saw her. She was standing, in a little white skirt, in the garden of a farmhouse, a cottage with crooked walls rather, and was decapitating dandelions with a stick. She was alone though she had, *has*, three elder siblings, also so-called contract children, one of whom nowadays is a director of the second-largest Swiss bank. She was really very small, yet already had the face she'd have later. The same smile, oscillating between affection and suspicion. I went up to the hedge — moved, as she looked so lovely, and furious, as she was cheating on me with another guy — and called,

'Isabelle!' She looked across to me, then lay into the flowers again. Now that someone was watching, she was hitting them more precisely, more powerfully, and several chopped-off yellow heads indeed fell to the ground.

'Look,' I said in French because Isabelle, who nowadays speaks German like pealing bells, wouldn't have understood me otherwise. 'I've a present for you.' She dropped the stick and came over to me at the fence and I bent down, kneeling slightly, until our faces were on the same level and very close, and gave her a neon sticker I'd actually wanted to give to my daughter. Her daughter. It was of an angry-looking Garfield, screaming that he never wanted to go to school again. Her blue eyes looked at me for a long time—we were very close, only the mesh of the fence was stopping me from kissing her—then she finally took my gift. I pushed it through the wire. Her mouth was smeared with jam and she was a little chinless, in a way I'd never noticed in the adult Isabelle. Her hair was blond, not brown! She looked at Garfield as if thunderstruck and I wanted to tell her that I was

Father Christmas, the Easter Bunny, that I knew the future and that hers had a few snowstorms in store, heartbreaking escapes, but then I'd come along! And I was just opening my mouth — I had to speak in a way she'd understand, and in French, into the bargain — when the cottage door opened and a woman became visible — my mother-in-law Alice, young, in a blue skirt with lots of white dots — and called, 'Isabelle! Viens tout de suite!' Her voice, so gentle in my experience, was as sharp as a scythe. Isabelle turned away from the fence and clomped through the grass and flowers that reached up to her chest. She had my sticker in her hand. Her mother, already calm again, was waiting for her with outstretched arms. Amused, I watched her too and when she passed a shack with two rabbits in it, I called over, 'I will marry you!' She turned back to me and waved. Alice watched with a smile that was trying to be polite, yet couldn't conceal her relief that I was finally going. When I reached the fountain, I turned round again. Alice was holding the sticker and looking at it, baffled. Isabelle was clinging to her skirt, pleading, her little hands

reaching for the gift she still wasn't getting back.
She began to cry, to scream, and both disappeared
into the house.

I cycled across a bog where peat cutters were
working in high boots, up to their knees in the
ground. Meadowfoam. Glistening water. Storks
and heron, snapping for frogs. Later, a little dog
trotted along behind me for a while, then suddenly
disappeared onto a side path. I sang, shouted with
glee and, at one point, recited a whole poem to the
Heavens. Swallows arced over me. On the horizon
were clouds, high towers. My Strand was moving
like on the first day of Creation. The pedal wasn't
yet scraping the chain case at every turn of the
wheel and the saddle, later an instrument of torture
with its many protruding springs, was a pleasant
leather cushion. Every now and then I overtook
a horse and cart. Cows on pastures. At one point,
a car with a wooden carburettor at the back
came towards me—the doctor, perhaps. Finally, I
reached a forest and, with it, the twilight of those
firs the demons hide under—the dwarfs and the
giants. It had got colder and, high above me, a

strong wind was swaying the treetops. Lynxes swept across the roadway, and weasels. I had to avoid the rough stones lying on the road. At one point, an old woman was sitting on a fallen tree, motionless, watching me go. Or had she *been* a tree stump? The birds above me were squawking now. For the first time, I realized I'd no idea how to get back to my old life, to Isabelle, to my daughter, into my house. Into my own present day. I realized I wanted to! I had a job to deliver in a few days! I loved the present! What was Isabelle doing right now? And my daughter, surely despairing without her father? What sense did it make to re-experience times I'd already put behind me? I knew, sure, who won the war, yet no one would believe me if I told them. If only I could recall the football results from back then at least! My father and I could've done the pools together. But I could only remember a game between the Swiss and the Dutch that had taken place shortly after the war, probably. At the age of about eight, I sat behind the goal — a privilege for children — and kept turning to try and see Papa who, just about crushed by the excited spectators, was standing on the terraces, also excited as we were winning in what was a wild frenzy, and Jacky Fatton scored the last of the seven goals from the corner flag, with an overhead kick, the like of which I've never seen again.

It had got dark meanwhile, mid-afternoon. Lightning flashed from the sky, thunder rolled, a storm raged and not far off was the sound of rain. I managed to keep dry. But felt cold and got a terrible fright when, out of nowhere, lightning struck close to me. A tree was burning. I continued, breathless, bent over the handlebars, praying without a proper faith in God, as I'm someone who only thinks to pray when I'm in for it. The firs formed a black corridor through which the road led, straight as a die. Lightning was now continuous—at times far off, often nearby. Finally, I reached a treeless plain and I felt like a rabbit, caught in the scope of celestial hunters. Was I crying? Soon though, no more St Elmo's fires were wandering along my handlebars, the storm was now raging over the Jura Mountains, accompanied by black downpours. I was still dry! Animal carcasses lay at the wayside.

Had the lightning struck them dead or was this a battlefield? I rode and rode and by the time I arrived outside my parents' house, my former home, night had really fallen. I was dripping with sweat. Put the bicycle against the Japanese tree — the helmet had disappeared — and went up the slab path to the front door, opened it, climbed the short staircase in the dark and entered the flat. No light in the hallway either but the living-room door was again ajar. Once again, a streak of light fell across my feet, this time without the rainbow colours. I could hear voices. My father was shouting agitatedly, my mother was sobbing. Simultaneously, a deep male voice spoke but was unable to calm my parents. I pushed the door open. My mother, in floods of tears, was on the couch, wringing her hands while my father had his back to me and was banging on the coffee table with both fists. The table wobbled on its thin metal stilts and cups and spoons and ashtrays slid back and forth as if on the high seas. Two men were perched in the armchairs. They looked like policemen and certainly were policemen as they had revolvers in their belts and were wearing completely identical suits, made from a rough, grey material. One, whom I immediately took to be the boss, was broad and heavy and had a neck like an ox whereas the other, who knotted his legs nervously, was more on the lean side. 'Do something!' my father roared. 'Would you finally damn well do something!'

'That one there knows him!' my mother exclaimed, spotting me. She jumped up and pointed at me. They all turned round.

'Who, me?' I stuttered. 'What? Your dog?'

'Our son!' my father shouted. 'He's disappeared, vanished without trace two days ago and these gentlemen are sitting on their fat arses and doing nothing!'

'You haven't given us the slightest lead that we as policemen can work on!' the lean one protested, jumping to his feet. 'He could be anywhere. At the North Pole, or somewhere very close.' He stood there, shaking, snorting, until the one with a neck like an ox pushed him back down onto his chair. He yawned.

'Lisette took him to the pictures the evening before last,' my father said, much more calmly. 'And when she went to fetch him, he was no longer there.' He noticed that he was smoking the filter of his cigarette and lit a new one.

'We've searched the cinema twice,' the lean one said, he too calm again. 'We didn't even find the toy car he had.'

'Do three-year-olds go to the pictures here?' I asked. 'Where I come from, the youngest are six, even when it's *Snow White*.'

'What do you mean "where I come from"?' The fat one I thought was the boss was suddenly wide awake. His anaemic apprentice spoke over him, though. 'We asked ourselves that too. Especially since the film seems to be of questionable pedagogical value. It's not on the education authority's list of recommended films, at any rate.'

'I told him so, there and then,' my mother sobbed, pointing at my father. 'He always thinks his son's grown up already. "If you do allow it," I said, "Lisette has to stay with him the whole time!"'

'You're always wiser after the event,' my father, immediately incensed, roared. He lit another cigarette while the officer with a neck like an ox set fire to a cheroot. I coughed, my mother coughed, the lean policeman coughed.

'I love him,' my mother said, eventually, flapping both hands to get rid of the fumes. 'I love my son.'

'I do too, I do too, or do you think I don't?' My father stubbed out both cigarettes in the senior policeman's cup—blind behind his wall of smoke, he didn't respond—took out a new packet of Parisienne, opened it and popped yet another cigarette in his mouth.

I felt—cataclysmic, it was—suddenly happy, charmed. Spreading my arms out, I said, 'I know where your son is!' Suddenly sure that I was hot on the trail of the answer to all the world's mysteries, I grabbed my father by the throat and roared in his ear that we'd find the little chap, the two of us. I laughed as my father got even redder in the face, as red as you can get, and he reached for my throat too and squeezed it too, so that we

40

were soon reeling around the room, like a dancing couple, my little father and me. He gasped, 'Really? Truly?' And I gasped, 'Most certainly!' My mother came crashing in from behind, grabbed my shirt and screamed that I was a murderer, a murderer, a murderer, until the one with the thick neck dragged himself up out of his armchair with a groan, flexed the fingers of both hands, as would a pianist about to play a difficult sonata, then let fly with an unannounced punch. He'd aimed at my chin but hit my father who, letting go of me, slid with a sigh to the floor. There he lay unconscious, his nose bleeding, while I stood astride him to pick up his cigarette and glasses. 'Murderer!' my mother shouted. This time, she meant the policeman.

A patch-job reconciliation followed and we were soon sitting round the table at the centre of which was now the coffee machine I knew only too well. A glass globe, the whole set-up made entirely of glass, with a spirit lamp burning beneath it. It looked like something from a chemistry lab. My father, his upper lip bedaubed with blood, was stirring the coffee sludge, bubbling in the uppermost funnel, with a much-too-small spoon. My mother was crying. The two policemen were staring at the miracle, this drink with an exotic aroma from countries from which goods no longer reached us for the longest time. Yes, throughout the war—and this war was happening now—my father had done everything, everything! to ensure he got his coffee. Sold off our meat and flour coupons, hawked our home-grown potatoes by the cartload, sold his own mother, or son. He was done stirring now—something he'd no doubt only done so thoroughly, like someone in love, in order to nose the wafting and rising aroma. He sat down again and watched, delighted, as the ready-to-drink coffee trickled slowly into the lower globe. I looked at him, suspicious. Had he traded me for a sack of unroasted Brazil special? It was clear to me though, of course, that if anyone, the ignorant policemen should pursue such a lead. I knew better. I'd often accompanied my father to a metalware shop on Schneidergasse where, conspiratorially, he whispered a secret code to the owner—'Five square-section keys for Dreyfus'—and was given a pre-packaged parcel for the price of which he should've received a whole crateful of square-section keys. Now we were all sitting there — breathing like boxers after a world-championship fight — listening to the wind rattling the windows.

'So you know where he is,' the senior policeman said, finally. 'Are you a fortune-teller?'

'Yes,' I said.

'You don't exactly look like one,' he muttered. 'Where is he then?' He took his cup and drank a sip of the coffee.

'Probably at my place,' I said. 'In my present. I . . .'

The policeman jumped up and, cursing, spat out his coffee onto his colleague's lap. The remains of my father's cigarettes had got into his mouth. The lean one looked, bewildered, at his now filthy uniform. Two coffee-soaked butts were sticking to his flies. My mother was wide eyed and my father, who had just removed his glasses to clean them, was blinking blankly.

'I know the future,' I continued. 'We'll win the war. Hitler will die a wretched death and with him, millions of others.'

'Right, I've had enough,' the one with the neck said, more to himself than to me. He was playing with his fingers again, each of which looked like a rubber truncheon. His eyes had become slits.

'I need Lisette,' I said, quickly. 'Just Lisette, then you'll have him back in no time.'

A few minutes later, Lisette was standing there, yawning. She'd been sleeping and had got dressed so quickly that her skirt was all crooked and her blouse buttoned the wrong way. Her hair was a red jumble. She looked at the chaos surrounding us, the blood on the floor, my battered father, the strange men. I felt calm and secure and wandered around the dear old room as my mother, my father and the two policemen started going on and on at Lisette. She was to trust them, they had to clutch at every straw, even this one. They all looked over to me. I, the straw, was standing in the niche where the table with my father's typewriter stood, a black monster, a Continental, with the

beginning of one of his pamphlets in it—peace to
the shacks and war on the kind of palace he lived
in. I don't know why but on a sudden impulse, I
removed the sheet of paper, crumpled it up
and threw it into the wastepaper basket. Books
everywhere. On all the walls. On a window-sill,
wooden figures from Africa with faces that looked
as if they were wearing gas masks—a man with an
erection with a shiny red tip and a woman whose
orifice was a white *v*. The gramophone was as big
as a trunk and yet smaller than I remembered.
Rugs. At the other end of the room stood a trolley
with metal wheels and beside it a cabinet with glass
doors. Suddenly, I saw it. My heart began to race.
There it was, the soda siphon bottle, on account of
which I'd undertaken this whole journey, that
gleaming blue soda siphon, up on top of the cabinet
and actually glistening—my father had turned the
light on out in the hallway. I walked across the
room, not taking my eyes off it, stood on tiptoe in
front of the cabinet and stared at the bottle. Its
glass gleamed when you were up-close, too.
Narrow grooves in which the light was refracted,

little air bubbles trapped in the glass, a little dirt also, here and there. I breathed. Next to the bottle lay slim capsules that were very dusty and beginning to rust. They went into the bottle top and released the carbon dioxide into the water. They were called bombs. Bombs like that, I'd once thought, fell out of the skies onto us humans, dealing out destruction. I'd never dared touch one. Now I raised a hand. I could take them, spirit them away. There'd be no more bombs. But, at that moment, my father called over, 'What are you waiting for?' and I lowered my hand again. 'Off you go!' In the doorway, I turned back. The soda siphon was floating above the cabinet, the glass front of which was also blue. I lifted my shoulders, a small shrug asking for forgiveness—I could see my blurred reflection—and, following my father, went down the stairs to join the others already at the front door. Behind streaks of cloud, a bright moon was sweeping across the sky as if it were being hounded out of the country. Lisette was wearing a raincoat she was holding shut at the collar with both hands. My mother was fixing her hair — Lisette's. The two policemen were standing in the bushes, one large shadow and one small, shuffling their feet.

'Don't disappoint us,' my father said, squeezing my hand. 'Adieu.'

'We won't see each other again,' I answered, holding his hand. 'Enjoy your cigarettes. Something will always kill us humans, one way or other.' My father smiled, nodded. He still had twenty-four years ahead of him. When the time came, mind you, he'd scream with pain and die wretchedly. I let go of his hand and said, 'Do you realize the manufacturer of your fags is an old Nazi?'

'Good God!' my father answered, smoking again, of course. He took the cigarette from his mouth, looked at it with a mixture of horror and regret — he'd hardly started smoking it — and stubbed it out on the wall of the house. 'I'll change brands!' My mother opened her mouth to speak but shut it again and began to scratch at the mark with her fingernails.

'You'll smoke Brunette instead,' I said. 'I know.'

'Come along,' the voice of the senior policeman said from the bushes. 'Get on with it!' his colleague piped up, like an echo.

I wanted to give my mother a kiss, the first kiss for an endless number of years, and the last, but she was so focused on the cigarette mark that I just left it. I could only see her behind, her hair and hear her scratching. I've already said how she died. She'd roared at the tram, I was later told, even at the point of her demise, insisting she was in the right. My father died much earlier, poorer, in the summer. His funeral took place in an oppressive heat. Many friends had come, in black, serious — people who liked to laugh so much too. There was no clergyman but one of the friends, a knobbly giant, gave a speech that had everyone in tears, me included, and then I waited with Isabelle at the bus stop and kissed her tears. She had to get to the station and I had to join the mourners for a snack in the cemetery restaurant. I'd only known Isabelle for two weeks and would never have expected her to travel from her distant town to join me and my dead father. She'd only been in his company once.

I'd left the two of them alone — I had to rush along to the postbox — and was hardly gone when my father began speaking a sparkling French to her as if *he* was the one in love. All my life, he'd had me believe that he knew no foreign languages. On our walks through the Jura, *I*'d had to ask the farmers if they had any milk and bread. In death, he had looked transparent and weightless though, when I wanted to move him onto his bed, I couldn't lift him. — I would've liked to tell my mother, I think, that I hadn't wanted to rescue the woman on the tower. But not now.

Like refugees, we swept down the path to the tram stop, in similar fashion to the moon. Lisette was still holding her coat shut and her steps were scattering the gravel. The dog — where did he suddenly come from? — was running riot round us, jumping on her and me, then disappeared, barking excitedly, into the darkness, only to turn up again like a torpedo. I turned round as I walked, two or three times, but couldn't see the policemen. They were probably applying all the finesse of their tiptoe training. At any rate, we then sat completely alone in an empty tram that turned up out of the night, entirely unexpected, with a little blue altar light at the front, a barely visible heavenly glow. The tram too was observing the blackout regulations. On the inside, though, it was bright and Lisette was certainly feeling a little safer — she was smiling now and glancing at me from time to time. I smiled back. I knew she had always drunk all the cod liver oil that was supposed to make me healthy and which she, unlike me, loved as others love syrup. I knew the smell of her breasts, her stomach — we'd rolled and tumbled in the grass often enough. The conductor, short of breath and over the age of retirement, gave her three white tickets on which the entire tram network was drawn and on which he clipped our destination with his puncher. The dog didn't know whether to sit beside her or beside me and was constantly changing seats. Once, on a tight bend at Tellplatz, he rolled as far as the door where he got tangled up in the conductor's legs. We had to laugh. Lisette too.

'We'll find him,' I said, 'I'm quite sure of it.'

'Are you from the police too?' Lisette, who knew some German after all, looked at me properly for the first time. Above her snub nose she had a few freckles that I remembered again, now that I saw her. Her eyes! And the hair that normally flowed over her shoulders and that, today, looked like a bivouac fire.

'No,' I said.

'I wish I could be at home,' she said. 'We've a farm. I'm the eldest of five sisters. I was always with the cows, out grazing. In the evening, my father would say, "Yes, I can rely on her, on Lisette." Now, I only get home at Easter and Christmas. We eat butter every day and eggs and bacon.'

When we got off again, I was sure the strategy of the two policemen had failed. The tram had probably left from under their noses. We went along a light-less street full of nooks and crannies, of mediaeval houses — Rheingasse, perhaps, or Spalenvorstadt — and nearly cannoned into lamp posts a few times and once into a man whose lit cigarette I saw only at the last minute. The moon was invisible, it had escaped successfully, probably.

Lisette stopped in front of a black building. We were there. Light escaped through the cracks in a door, behind it noisy voices. 'What now?'

'I'll go in and you wait. He'll come out with the rest of the audience and tell you all about the film on the way home.'

She looked at me. The beam of light from the cinema fell on her face, her eyes, and of course I kissed her. She didn't resist. On the contrary, she'd been waiting for a kiss. She leant into me. 'I've loved you, Lisette,' I whispered in her ear, this time in French, 'for forty-nine years.' She pressed herself twice as hard against me in reply and wrapped her arms round my neck. We stumbled across the pavement like two drunks, biting each other, eating each other, and almost fell. Then stood against the wall, between the bicycles. My tongue licked round her ears, her mouth, her nose, while her fingers were all over me. Then, though, while my hands were still doing the opposite — hers were doing much more — I broke away and rushed, without looking back, to the door and the box office. Had I not done so, we'd have been lost. My parents without a son,

Isabelle a widow, my daughter an orphan and Lisette burdened with a lifelong guilt. I purchased a ticket and was surprised to find in my pocket one of the currently valid, old-fashioned banknotes. Had Lisette slipped it to me? Inside, boys and girls were clambering about the now shoddy plush chairs, making a rumpus. Hardly any adults. None actually. I sat down right at the front as always and was alone again. Or rather, Jimmy, the dog, was with me. He'd taken the opportunity to scamper through the gap in the door. I couldn't help him any more now. Like Napoleon on the battlefield of Austerlitz, he was sitting on the next seat, looking ahead, as if he knew that the most exciting things were about to happen there. I petted him. The light went out and the projector displayed the credits and opening images on the screen.

The film was an animated cartoon but not a Disney, the girls weren't lovely enough and the animals not sweet enough for that. It told of the life of a dark-skinned boy from Bangladesh or India — I couldn't tell the exact difference now either — who, at first, lived in the countryside and was carried on his mother's back as she walked along behind gaunt oxen. Sunsets, and mother and son, sitting cheek-to-cheek. Then the mother died and the father sat sadly beside the similarly dead oxen—they'd starved to death—and took the boy, who could now walk, and moved to the city with him. Bombay or Tahorehuhu. The boy prowled the streets, begging, got bigger and was soon an experienced pickpocket. Still a child, he joined a radical political group whose goal was to bomb the English out of the country. They had a low opinion of Gandhi and of facing the British cannons with their bare chests. At their behest, which he misunderstood—he was twelve, remember—he shot a British subject dead, a very young woman from Southampton, who was on her honeymoon and knew nothing about politics except that the British were the noblest creatures under the sun. The boy shouldn't have murdered her at all but rather the wife of the governor of the district, as his representative, because the governor himself, a sinister type, was always surrounded by his guards.

Anyway, the boy got older, became an adult. His father died. He now lived alone on the roof of the house where his father had once lodged, and it was so suited for all kinds of escapes that the police would wander around for months in the corridors and stairwells and finally leave as skeletons. One mild evening, he met an English tourist, a philanthropist, who liked India—if it really wasn't Suriname—better than the Empire and they drank raki together, or whatever is drunk there, whisky, probably, and the boy didn't rob the Englishman, didn't kill him on the way home either, and they saw each other again and again and again. In the end they were so close that the man took the boy, who was twenty meanwhile, or older, to England, where he provided him with an education that, because he was talented, breathtakingly talented, took him, via school qualifications, caught up on in night shifts—incredible examiners, in gowns, who then had to give the brown-skinned stranger an A-plus in all his subjects after all—to Oxford where he was soon Number One in the most prestigious college and the coxswain of the famous rowing eight that, in his day, won every contest with the boat from Cambridge, also because he weighed fifty kilos, max. The enemy's cox, the son of the principal, was a fatty. The boy did his doctorate and took to writing and, dipping into the pot of gold from his youth, published one book after the other and just as his benefactor died—an old man meanwhile and a Nestor in the House of Lords—he published a work that caused such an almighty stir, attracted so much jubilation and indignation that he had to hide from both his enemies and admirers. They wanted either to kiss him to death or to kill him. Now *he* was the victim. He spent a few years in cellars and attics until he could no longer stand living like that and left his refuge and went to a cinema. He couldn't have cared less. He watched the film, the images flickering like his cerebral cortex itself, and when he stepped outside again he was in his old city, his former time, and he looked for the house that, indeed, was still standing where it always did—his father, a young man, his mother, however, well and truly dead—and *he* stayed, he didn't look for a way back, also because his father wasn't especially missing his little son who had vanished that very

evening. It looked more like he was glad to be rid
of the wastrel. Similarly, the old man, who had
been the boy, settled down at his old place with his
nanny from back then, a neighbour, a destitute girl
with beautiful eyes, who helped him to mesmerize
and fleece anyone seeking help and who lay with
him at night and danced and cavorted on him, and
he was happier than he had ever been. Laughing,
he sometimes said, when his ecstasy had left him
unthinking and careless, that people were after
him, were scouring every corner of his homeland
for him and yet all they had to do was wait for the
small matter of forty or fifty years and he'd be
back. It was all double Dutch, true, to the nanny,
a sixteen-year-old girl, but her lover's every word,
even if it was double Dutch, was music to her ears.
All fortune-tellers, he said, were in reality
returnees. That is why they knew so much. She,
for instance, in ten years' time, would marry a
master butcher. 'Let's make the most of it till then,
darling.' The nanny laughed and shook her head
but, naturally, the master butcher did come along
and got her pregnant countless times, and the

young woman couldn't comprehend her fate though she idolized her children and revered her husband and couldn't forget the old man, who was really old meanwhile. From time to time, she'd creep up onto his jumble-of-houses roof and let him tell her her future — it didn't look good, so the fortune-teller lied to her — and then she lay with him though that's a mortal sin in India, and Pakistan too, and only went back down at sunset, alone — she knew all the different routes. Once, she found her husband who had followed her into the corridors and, for a few moments, played with the idea of letting him continue to stray. She then took him by the hand after all and led him outside where they never mentioned the incident again, never again.

At the end, the film became a kind of documentary, not animated any more but filmed in black and white, with sound, even. There were subtitles too, Indian however, or Tibetan, which seemed rather pointless to me in a film for three-year-olds. It wasn't for three-year-olds. It wasn't even for children. My father had got it wrong again.

Dazed, I got up when the light came back on in the cinema and floated out with the other children who, this time, had all stayed and were now shell-shocked and silent. My heart was beating violently after all. It had become colder. It was night now too and for a terrible moment I thought I'd landed back with Lisette. Then, though, I saw that lights were shining everywhere. Adverts were flashing, all different colours, trams rushed past, and cars. Cars, cars and more cars. I was back in my town. All the same, I hurried much too quickly up Rämistrasse, which was one great building site and also aflame. Jimmy, good little Jimmy, was running along beside me and to take my mind off my excitement I told him the story of the film he'd seen himself. I explained to him that there was no dog in the story, that he was an accident and would just have to accept his fate. The traffic this time, at Heimplatz, was chaotic. I waited for minutes at a red light, holding the dog by the collar. The cars nose to tail. The moon was back again, fifty years older and not looking any different. As I approached my house I was so excited I could see nothing but stars. I raced up the stairs — the right door, the wrong door, I didn't know — to find Isabelle and Mara sitting at the dinner table. Instantly, the stars were gone. They were bent over a Garfield magazine and Mara, imitating the fat tabby, was reading out a punchline. They barely raised their heads as I stepped up to the table. 'Hello!' Isabelle said but she was looking at Garfield or Odie or Jon and Mara said nothing at all, just started to tackle the next story in which the lazy brute was lying in a box and had something against it being Monday again. Mara burst into mad laughter when she saw Jon's — the cat's owner's — face with lasagne sticking to it. 'Hello!' I said, sitting down. I was breathing more calmly but noticed my shirt was all sweaty.

Then, though, Jimmy barked. This time too he'd managed to bolt through the door with me. Isabelle leapt up and Mara sat there, open-mouthed. I grinned sheepishly and shrugged. The dog had jumped onto my lap and looked like Odie, the comic-strip dog. He had the same idiotic look in his eyes, the same long, panting tongue and pricked-up ears. 'What's all this?' Isabelle screamed, completely changed. Mara shouted, 'Swe-e-e-e-t,' rushed over to Jimmy, petted and kissed him and asked, 'Is he for me?' When I nodded, she flung her arms round me. Isabelle stood there, speechless, staring at the monster that was now dancing around with Mara, barking more and more excitedly with every little jump.

'He followed me home,' I said. 'He has no one but me.'

'I know a boy,' Mara exclaimed. 'He has the exact same one!'

'You know that dogs and I . . .' Isabelle muttered, pale, and with tears in her eyes. She sat down again, shaking her head in despair.

'But Garfield!' I said. 'You do like him!'

'Funny, eh?' She was smiling now after all. 'He's actually rather daft. I don't know why but every time I see him a strange feeling goes through me as if I were a child again.'

'His dog tag is ancient!' said Mara, who had grabbed Jimmy's collar and had her eyes right up against it. 'It's from 1941!'

'Write and tell the *Guinness Book of Records*,' I said. 'You've got the oldest terrier in the world. Fifty years old. At least.'

'Probably just his owner being sentimental,' Isabelle said. 'Gives each new dog—when the old one dies—the collar of their first pooch. Whose dog is it anyway?'

'Mara's,' I said.

'Be serious for once. You're always making jokes.'

'My parents' then.'

Isabelle looked at me, furious? no, amused, more like. She was indeed a little chinless. Still had the same crafty eyes. She poured herself some wine and, seeing the look I gave her, poured me some too. We raised our glasses and drank. 'I'm always making jokes!' I said. 'Ha ha!' Isabelle waved, as if to say, 'Don't bother. It's all right,' or something along those lines. The wine, a Rioja, did more than just wet our throats.

'How was the film?' Isabelle asked.

'Mad,' I answered. 'One question, in this respect. How long was I actually gone?'

'Three hours or so,' Isabelle said. 'Is your watch broken?'

'Was,'—I hesitated, didn't know myself what I was exactly asking—'a boy here? Did you two happen to see a little boy, of about three, at all?'

'No,' said Isabelle. But Mara, who had pushed the dog onto its back and was rubbing its stomach, called over, 'Didn't I tell you? The one with the dog. With Jimmy. He was loitering around the house the whole time. At one point, I went down and gave him a chewing gum. Suddenly, he was gone.'

'He went home,' I said.

Mara rummaged in her pockets and revealed a small red toy car. 'He gave me that for it.' My fire engine! It even had its ladder on the roof, the ladder it later lost. 'That's nice,' I said.

I finished my drink, put my hands on Isabelle's, looked at her and mumbled, 'One more thing.' I looked across to Mara to see if she was listening. But she was dragging the dog by the tail across to the record player to play him her newest CD, some pounding guitar stuff by her favourite band that, on the cover, looked like a bunch of fascist murderers. The dog yelped excitedly when he felt her headphones on his head — in the evening, you see, if we manage to have our way, we don't permit any more droning heavy metal — and, when Mara pressed 'play', he leapt into the air like a scalded cat. Stormed off until the headphone cable suddenly stopped him. Mara clapped her hands, 'This is great, Dog, isn't it?'

'Your human affectivity group,' I said, quietly, to Isabelle, 'are there men in it?'

'Of course. Holger, Jürgen and Paul.'

'And?' I hesitated. 'How do you get on with them?'

'Why?'

'Nothing. This Holger, for instance.'

'He's a bit of a dick.'

'Yeah?' I felt myself going red. 'And the others?'

'To be honest,' suddenly, she was warming to the topic, 'we've even thought about forming a women-only group. You can't imagine what rubbish those three come out with sometimes.'

I nodded. I nodded and nodded. Laughed suddenly. Pulled Isabelle out of her chair and danced around the room with her. Swayed her to and fro, shouting with glee. Isabelle looked baffled, then laughed too and started spinning me around. Mara immediately switched her media tower onto loudspeaker and took Jimmy's headphones off. My good mood had come over me like a thunderstorm. I stamped my feet and raved, like one possessed. Mara charged up, wanted to dance with me and the dog jerked in and out between our legs. Somehow the cat had got in too and was jumping across the tables and chairs. The walls were trembling, Mara, of course, had turned up her system full blast.

Much later—we'd danced for quite a long time, till we were out of breath—Isabelle and I were at the table again. Mara had fallen asleep on the floor and Jimmy was licking her face. The cat was on a cushion, pretending not to notice him. We'd opened a new bottle of Rioja. The moon was looking in through the window. A clear sky with a few clouds. We talked about this and that. 'Today was a long day!' I mumbled finally, yawning. Isabelle nodded.

'You know,' she said, 'basically, I like dogs. When I was little, I once got a sticker from my mother, there was a dog on it, a fat mutt, yellow. Gorgeous.'

We stood up, put our glasses in the sink and the empty bottle with the others. While Isabelle carried Mara to bed, I made a basket for Jimmy and sat him in it. 'Be good and sleep!' I told him. Then I went downstairs and, as I always do before bed, cast a glance at the manuscript I was working on. Something was very strange—no paper in the typewriter and the wrong page at the top of the pile beside it. 'Who was tidying up in here?' I called upstairs. 'I'll knock their head off!' But I was too tired, or too happy, to do so. Isabelle and I got into bed, kissed a little, yawning, and fell asleep. I don't know what Isabelle dreamt of. I, at any rate, didn't dream.

That bomb, incidentally, that looked like the siphon capsules on the blue cabinet, was called Little Boy. I'd often thought of it, of that fat metal egg. I'd often thought that I could've been living in Hiroshima, that I lived there, for back then, in the years and days before, it was no big deal to live in Hiroshima. People lived in Hiroshima like people lived in Dresden or Zurich, simple as that. And then, on a day like any other, on the last day, we were outside the house, in the garden, looking up into the sky, into a blue sky, in which we could see, very small it was, a single shiny plane veering off at that precise moment. We didn't think anything of it. We didn't think that this plane had just dropped Little Boy, a siphon capsule, for we couldn't see Little Boy who was starting to fly at us at the speed of free fall. We still had time. We still have time, lots of time, my mother said to me. Take that stone out of your mouth, it's bad for you. We could see the black bomb now, Little Boy, if we were to look up, but we don't look up, I look at my friend, whom I don't remember, and say to him that . . . THAT . . . Ever since, his silhouette has been etched on the wall of my house. I have vanished. My friend has vanished. My mother has vanished. We don't exist any

more. Many people don't exist any more. Many
people won't exist any more.

2

Years ago, when I was so small that everyone could see me, about three years old, I stood, bloated with happiness, on the windowsill in my room, looking out into the world. My mother beside me was just as amazed. 'There! — there!' we exclaimed, clapping our hands. Birds flew out of a glorious sky, arced round us and vanished into the blue, as if it were porous or had secret holes. My mother and I looked at each other, flabbergasted, flabbergasted and excited. Far off was that tower full of invisible water and even further back, hills bordered the horizon. A field full of cornflowers and poppies. I'd been wakened, when the sun climbed over the horizon, by the buzzing of bees and the chirping of birds, that wonderful racket, their scratching and scraping on the blind casing above my bed. Though it was early enough for the dew still to be glistening on the blades of grass, my mother was already working among the beans, spraying them with a blue fog she pumped from something akin to a rucksack. Even her hands were blue. I ran around in what she sprayed, became blue too and watched the blue-powdered mice fleeing on their network of paths to the nearest hole. To be a mouse! There were cats, of course — we had a few too — but they had the dogs that chased them up into trees. I even badgered ours, Jimmy, the terrier, who wouldn't harm a fly. Barking, he swept up behind one of the cats that retreated to the lowest bough of an apple tree without really running. I laughed and danced and waved to the sun. Crawled through the bushes and spoke to rabbits. My mother was now at the water barrel, filling watering cans. I went to her, held onto her skirt, also when she went over to the tomatoes and watered them. I smelt the odourless still-green fruit, the leaves. Only when I had really wet legs did I toddle back to the barrel and remove moss from the beams on which it stood. Fragrant moss, with beetles scrabbling in it. Underneath was earthy, full of roots and worms. 'Look over there, the stork,' my mother called and I saw it heading for the horizon, its neck stretching far ahead. The sun was now high in the sky and had turned yellow. I leapt along the path, from slab to slab, without my feet touching the grass growing between them. No dew on the stalks now. The stones were so hot, I had to keep moving. Lizards darted off, and I lay in wait for a long time before a cavity in the wall and finally saw a head in the purple shade, attentive eyes, an agile tongue. Then the whole lizard ventured out into the sun — it thought I was a piece of nature — and I looked at its scaled neck, its skin swelling to the rhythm of its heart. When I tried to catch it, it was faster than my hand, of course, and disappeared in a flash among the lavenders. I stood up, brushed the pine needles and pebbles from my knees and crawled along the hedge through the thick rambling bushes, hidden to all members of the adult tribe, on this occasion three old ladies who, chattering to one another, dragged themselves to a bench beyond the hedge at the furthest edge of the garden where they then discussed their afflictions. 'Brain tumour!' 'Physiotherapy!' 'Diarrhoea!' Holding my breath, I lay so close behind them I could have reached out and touched them. I noted every detail. In the field, the farmer was working with his horses and further away still, the gamekeeper emerged from the hazelnut bushes with his rifle. I jumped up, fought my way through the grove—didn't matter what happened to the ladies—and ran up the stairs in the house, as far as the attic, where soldiers now lodged and no one was allowed. Even my mother was forbidden to go up. The military rule didn't apply to me. I moved around the attic flat, now converted into an office, as if I were at home here, crawled under the tables and got an apple from an officer, a fat man with white hair. Another one was sitting on a table, reading papers. Outside on the roof terrace crouched a soldier with his back against the aerial that looked like a ship mast. He was peering through a telescope over into Markgräflerland and Alsace — our house was at the highest point in the canton, even higher than the water tower. Far below, my mother was crouching among the pota- toes, pulling weeds out, and the soldier adjusted the telescope so I could see her up-close, her face that didn't know I could see every fleck on the skin, every wrinkle, that it was as big as the moon for me. She was moving her lips as if in prayer. I tried, without success, to read them. My friend then helped me to find the gamekeeper — without the telescope, I spotted a small version of him under a cherry tree and pointed him out, all excited. The soldier laughed once he'd tracked him down. 'There you are, look! Your monster!' The gamekeeper was peeing against a tree — steady stream, red skin — and tilted his head back as the smoke from the pipe in his mouth was tickling his nose. His rifle was stood against a tree. I moved the telescope across to the enemy, the murderers, where things were as quiet as they were here, even quieter. Houses, trees, meadows, close enough to touch, not a soul to be seen until, suddenly, a man with a horse and cart came out of a barn and disappeared round a corner. The Rhine was flashing and glistening and flowed into the sky. The block that was Istein, a fort armed with canons, was glowing in the sun. The Elsace lay beneath a veil of mist. Not a sound anywhere, just the hiss of a match when the soldier lit a cigarette. A telephone rang. One of the officers spoke briefly, then hung up. I ran a stick along the broad, grey, grille perforations of the railings round the terrace until the white-haired officer stuck his head out of the door and said, 'That's enough, little man. Why don't you go down to your Mama and get us a few tomatoes and a chunk of bread.' So I slid down the stairs on my bum, opening and closing my legs like scissors. By the time I reached the bottom, I'd forgotten the tomatoes. I went to the toilet, the edge of which was nearly up to my chin, then couldn't get the door open, so started to cry, roaring until Lisette came and said, 'Mais quoi?' and 'Ça ne va plus, non?' or words to that effect. She was wearing a blouse with red polka dots, put my socks and shoes on — her hair blazing before my eyes — and we set out on our long, long way to the tower, a walk we did once a day because, she thought, I had other children to play with there. She, at any rate, liked to sit with her girlfriends on a wall and chat. She was way ahead of me this time too, calling back 'Mais viens!' while I bent over a dried-up earthworm and, with a stick, scratched out a face in the dust on the road. My shoes — sandals with crossed leather straps — were powdered white. Chamomile was growing and I had to crush it between my fingers, of course, and smell it! A stag beetle was crawling between the blades of grass and when I got up again, Lisette had arrived at the battery, that fortress where there was no danger, it was more of a raised park actually, and down its steep grassy side I then slid. Lisette waved to her friends who were supervising their charges at the — now near — tower. I played hopscotch with them, looking up the white wall of the tower as I hopped. At the top, heads were bent over the railings round the terrace. I pulled and pulled at Lisette, tore her skirt to rags nearly until, finally, still turned to a friend, she said, 'mais oui, mais oui,' then came with me, put a coin into a slit and pushed her way into the tower through a creaking turnstile while I climbed in between the metal bars. Cool, almost damp air. The staircase was steep and never-ending. I ran ahead, full of zeal, yet still had to be carried up the last hundred steps. At the top, we stood gaping down at what was below. I had my arms round Lisette's neck so tightly that she said, 'allons, Croquignol,' she wasn't about to throw me down, was she. Our house had turned into a dice. It stood in the fields, looking quite strange, as if a giant had lost his toy. The soldier on the roof had become a black dot, leaning against his mast, and my mother, looking very small, was walking over to the walnut tree. Jimmy was jumping up on her, a flea. I wanted back down to earth and home. Lisette gave in and carried me on her shoulders, singing French songs and taking huge donkey-like leaps. I was thrown this way and that and screamed with pleasure. At home, my mother set me down in the potatoes and gave me a beaker to put the beetles into. I put in one or two, watched how they climbed the sides, then when they reached the rim, shoved them back into the abyss with some grass. One I threw into the air but it was too daft to fly away and dropped like a stone among the plants. I then watched one of his friends eating a hole — much bigger than itself — into a leaf. Suddenly, my father came running through the garden in his soldier's uniform and with such a red face I hardly recognized him. He didn't see me. I dropped the beaker and swept in behind him, calling, 'Papa! Papa!' His steel helmet lay at the front door and on the stairs I gathered up the leather straps and his ammunition belt and bayonet. Inside the flat, I followed a clothes trail as far as the bathtub where my father was standing, stark naked, holding the shower hose over his head. In the doorway, in her gardening clothes and with Papa's cigarette between her fingers, my mother was hopping up and down and shouting as he wouldn't have heard her otherwise with the noise of the water. 'Are you on leave?' — 'No!' — I shouted something too and, when no one answered, put on the helmet that was so big I disappeared beneath it, its rim landing on my feet. I blundered around, clattering into the furniture. In the bathroom things had—long since—gone all quiet, in the whole flat, even, and I stopped and pricked up my ears and upon hearing nothing, absolutely nothing, I counted first to one hundred, then to a thousand and sang 'Ladybird, Ladybird,' the German version, and wondered where Pomerania was, telling myself really far away, for sure. Finally, the door to my parents' room opened and my father and my mother were back again. My father snatched the helmet off me—'Ah! there you are!'—and called, 'Lisette! Lisette!' My mother, barefoot now and in her underskirt, had eyes only for Papa. Her hair was down, flowing like a waterfall down to her hips. I ran into the living room, took the soda siphon bottle from the coffee table and when my mother followed me, sprayed her from head to toe. She squealed and, laughing, took the bottle from me. It gleamed in all the colours of the rainbow. Scolding me but in the best of moods, she refilled it with water, screwed a new bomb into the neck of the bottle and put it on top of the cabinet with the blue glass door. In the hallway, my father was leaning over Lisette, speaking into her ear, and Lisette was looking at him, chuckling with pleasure. She nodded, blushing all over, pulled my socks up, tapped my trousers — a cloud of dust — and before I knew it, we were out on the street. I'd only just managed to grab my fire engine and now ran it along every hedge and every wall. 'Where are we going?' 'To the pictures,' Lisette said. 'You're getting to go to the pictures. Your father's letting you see a great film.' She chuckled again and took even bigger steps, such that my arm got even longer and I twirled behind her like a paper kite along the dirt track leading to the tram stop. The sun went down beyond the crop fields, colouring me red. Lisette's hair too was glowing more than ever. Next thing, we were sitting in the tram and I was running my engine to and fro on the wooden seats.

Not until we were in the cinema — I'd never been in one before — did I notice that Lisette had left me on my own. I got up on my seat and looked here and there but the many other children in the hall prevented me from going to look for her. The film also started almost immediately, an out-of-focus shimmering to begin with, a fog from which only slowly—the man in the projection cabin was probably turning his lenses in a very leisurely fashion—a landscape emerged, paddy fields, in which oxen were moving, led by a boy with a straw hat. A bit further back was the tower of a pagoda. The film showed the life of this boy who, I have to say, when he could be seen in close-up a little later, resembled me so much I cried out and the children to my right and left became aware of me and, whispering, pointed at me though the boy in the film had much darker skin and black eyes. Besides, the film was in black and white. My heart began to race. In the India or Siam up on the screen, a war was taking place. Monsters with tanks were raging beyond the horizons, smashing world empires and swallowing peoples but here, in the paddy fields, there was a deep peace. Clouds in a high sky, the babble of water, bamboo-flute music and here and there a neighbour who, in the distance, rowed past in a boat, waving. The boy and his mother, a dainty woman with a red dot on her brow, slept in a reed hut without the boy's father—he was mentioned only once, as if in passing—who guarded a railway bridge in distant Manchuria or observed through his binoculars a plain across which the wind drove clouds of dust. When the boy was not with the oxen or his mother—and they always stayed close—he'd hop along the paths between the rice ponds, watch frogs and water fleas and, on one occasion, the gamekeeper who had caught a rabbit—his paws had a firm hold of its hind legs and he was banging it on the stones in the path. The boy froze with fright and the gamekeeper grinned and showed the boy the bleeding head of the rabbit.

But soon the sun was shining again and the boy was hunting out heron that flew off clumsily. He accompanied his mother into the rice that, for him, was a deep lake in which he was up to the chin in water when he had to pick the worms off the plants. Between his legs swam fish. Suddenly, he could see his father running across the dyke that led from the roadway to their house, as if he were escaping from something, and by the time the boy too had reached the reed hut his father was minus his uniform and sword and over his mother, who wasn't naked, it's true, but oddly wasn't defending herself, rather, following all the father's movements with her eyes shut and her mouth open, rolling beneath him and sighing, such that the boy, and with him every child in the cinema, couldn't shout, Papa! Papa! and certainly not, Mama! Instead, they lowered their eyes and turned away, just like the camera which—the sighing still audible from a fair distance—focused on the floor, the father's loincloth and sandals, then accompanied the boy behind the hut where he decapitated water lilies with Papa's sword. The father later stepped out of the hut, with the mother looking out from under the arms he held out to the sun, a cloth round her body that did not, however, cover one breast. Her hair flowed over her skin. The boy jumped up to his father who kissed him and threw him up in the air. And the last time, he threw him too high or at too much of a slant, so that he didn't catch him again at any rate and the boy fell into the rice. Everyone laughed. Like a drowned rat and covered in mud, he stepped back onto land. It turned out his father had left the war without permission, had left his long since decimated bunch of loyalists whose job it was to creep through the night and set the enemy's trucks alight. I'll be shot one way or other, the father said. Both of you, I wanted one last time just to—. The mother implored him not to return to certain death but the father charged off, tying his sword round him as he ran. The mother stood there for a long time, her raised hand as if frozen above her, but the boy was soon sitting on an ox, like a sultan on the back of his elephant.

Again, the sun shone every day. Again, he woke every morning, excited, looking forward hugely to all that the day might bring. He stood outside the hut, breathing the wind, ordered the red sun to rise over the horizon and turn yellow and it did. He whittled a flute from a bamboo cane and played on it. Caught colourful salamanders. Ate berries. Climbed up the pagoda, whose wood grated, and looked down on the round headgear of the farmers in the fields, on the oxen that seemed to swim in the water, on the green huts dotted round the tiny islands in the great deal of water. The horizons were bordered by hills. In the evenings, he snuggled up to his mother who clasped him to her bosom and kissed him to sleep whereas she herself lay awake, looking up at the reed ceiling, watery-eyed.

But then the war was over and after an evening full of Chinese lanterns and the hum of gnats, when the rice farmers had danced and shouted with glee, the father came home too. He'd not been killed. The boy became sick, caught a fever, could see ghosts creeping around, murderers, and his parents had to sit by his bed and promise him he wasn't dying. Despite their assurances, he saw them—though they were sitting beside him, wiping his brow—turn into sugarloaves and float above the paddy fields, dissolve into thin air. A single wave and they'd have been washed away.

Now his grandmother, his mother's mother, was also living in their hut—a saintly old woman, nothing but wrinkles and skin, who sat on a mat all day with her legs knotted behind her head. She stank of faeces and tobacco and took up more than half the space with her rituals. One morning, the boy was playing beside the tower and suddenly the farmers working nearby, men and women alike, were screaming and staring up at the sky, and the boy took one step to the side and looked up too and a black shadow crashed to the ground right beside him. A peasant woman had jumped from the tower and would have slain him had he stayed where he'd been. A young woman. It turned out that she'd just tearfully told the saintly grandmother she loved a farmer but he had chosen another and she'd tried to convey her suffering in a story about a swan and a panther but that hadn't eased her suffering and now if the Good Woman didn't help her she was going to jump from the tower. The saint in the hut had said nothing, simply nothing. She was someone who thought that human beings are in any case on their way to blissful oblivion and to nothing else and that no one has the right to stop them. That said, she herself clung doggedly to this earthly life, tied herself, now and then, into new physical knots and, if the boy wasn't watching, walked on her hands over to the food plate quick as a flash and gobbled up his rice ration. She didn't ever propose to die and be burnt on a pyre. Instead, the boy surprised his mother a short time later, as she lay curled on the ground behind the hut, whimpering and biting a cushion. His father was standing awkwardly beside her. This time, the saint, the grandmother, did open her mouth and spoke in an ancient language and healers applied leeches all over his mother's body. His father looked out over the water. The rice rotted away and the oxen died. One morning, on the eve of which the boy had thought nothing of note, his mother was dead. Stiff, cold. She was bewailed — by distraught women, the old lady was still the loudest, though — and cremated and, in the distance, his father walked among the wretched rice plants, stumbling into waterholes and not eating.

The boy now thought, where on earth has this wonderful world gone? What has happened? The world still looked as it had before but he'd become suspicious. There was a swindle going on. But where? The frogs were the same as before, they were croaking as they always did, they couldn't be blamed. The bamboo canes and the sword lilies were innocent too. The neighbours' huts couldn't help it either and it wasn't their fault if the boy fiddled around with matches once and set first a little grass, then a bush and finally a whole house alight. He stamped around in the flames, then ran off and, from the roof of the pagoda, saw all the people rushing up, trying to put the flames out and the hut turning to ashes. No one sussed that he'd started the fire. His father said the heat was to blame, that there was such a heat that year, houses were going up in flames by themselves. Soon, the paddy fields would be burning too. The neighbours nodded.

The boy came to the conclusion finally that the visible world is a swindle. His theory was: someone had an interest in children—and not just children—believing, though it wasn't true, that life in this world was magnificent. But the opposite was the case. This someone, the god wept for by his grandmother, perhaps, that snake-legged, multi-headed, undivided god, had maliciously built the visible world before the eyes of his future victims to lull them into a sense of security so that he could be more certain of being able to devour them later. He'd not overlooked a single detail. Not the swallows, not the lotus, not the ever-changing clouds. Such beauty was lost on *him*, *he* didn't need it but it tied *us* to him. If the boy now walked among the paddy fields, he held his hands out in front like a blind man, for he was sure that only when he lingered where divine expectation wanted him to be was the beautiful world so real and so unspeakably carefully worked out. So inconceivably tempting. And he was sure that somewhere this beautiful world had a limit—every step he took beyond his daily radius might lead him there, to this wall, a mural, on which the rest was painted, more generously, more roughly, intended to be viewed from afar. Anyone not paying attention or walking too quickly could knock their brains out. Blood stains, at that point, on the mural. That said, the boy entertained the idea too that this mural of the world might be something more like a sky-high film, a wall of light plonked in the landscape, through which everyone who reached it could then walk. With a single, unexpected step, every mortal would enter the netherworld, its secrets would no longer be concealed from us. Maybe his mother was walking around in there somewhere, her arms held out too, and the boy, the singer, by singing, could lead her back to the world of the living, to the beautiful swindle. I was glad I wasn't in his shoes, that I had a mama. Maybe that's why, for a while, I didn't pay proper attention but peered, left and right, at the children, and so missed how and where the boy found the entrance to the otherworldly world. The crack. Suddenly, at any rate, he was standing before the folds of a curtain and looking down into a dull landscape. Into gloomy light. Up at a sky made of crude oil and tar, it seemed. A steep path led down into a valley, at the end of which blue light flared. Stones, rubble, and when the boy started to take a few steps down, the pebbles slid with him such that, despite his desperate efforts to go back, he ended up further down. And so he went where the scree took him. Vapours were coming from below though it wasn't hot. He didn't see any people, couldn't see them — saw no one, not a soul — and then suddenly he did, for he was walking on them, on the dead from all times, on skulls and bones and remains that had become hills and mountains and groaned beneath his feet. Stones, pebbles, white dust. Sometimes though a mouth grinned up from the desert floor or an empty eye socket watched. Finally, he came to a rock pulpit from which he looked down. Creatures were moving, walking to and fro! He didn't have a harp but he did have his flute and if he saw anyone he loved, he'd certainly want to play on it. The shadows, mind you, were then all strangers. Men, women, walking in cold mourning. A child, maybe three years old, tried to give its mother—lying on her back, burnt to a cinder, her mouth open—a clod of earth to eat. Other shadows stood by a pit, then tumbled into it. A man fled, leaving a shoe on the path, with the stump of a leg and its sock sticking out. From a railway carriage, the side of which was opening, rumbled bodies. Somewhere a pile of spectacles, millions of pairs of spectacles, all the same kind, round, with a fine metal frame. Somewhere else hats. People suspended on hooks. People impaled on metal stakes. People on the ground, their heads smashed to bits. The children looked at him. Only they did, but all of them, even those without eyes, those consumed by fire, those with bloated stomachs, those clinging to the necks of their dead mothers or fathers. They all looked at him so much he closed his eyes, or I closed mine, and with me all the children in the cinema, so much that we started to scream, to screech, so much that, red-faced, we danced around on our seats, pushing and shoving one another. When I finally looked to the front again, the boy was walking through the light, flames that made him feel cold. He ended up in a grey meadow, crashed to the ground, exhausted, and sang—squawked, more like—a song about a white bird and a leopard-like animal, the favourite playmates of the princess of a large kingdom. The flute played itself beneath his trembling fingers. The princess loved a prince. Gave him, to win him over, first the leopard, then the bird and finally dived into a black pond, never to resurface. The prince, only now, and too late, realized what he'd lost and dived in after the princess. Swimming, he reached a grove where the dead stroll and where he stood before the assembled other-siders and sang so purely, so beautifully, that the dead permitted the lovers to return to life, and so the prince led the princess up the steep path to the sun and became her king and both slept in the same bed by night and ate the same bread by day. Their subjects became the happiest of people and painted a leopard and a dove on their crest. Thus sang the boy, thus played his flute, and when they were done the dead in hell were standing round him, just as dead as before, and the children were still burnt to cinders, the murdered impaled on their stakes and hanging on their electric fences and lying in the cellars or curled up in the snow or the mud of a field with no horizon. The boy threw his flute into the grass and climbed the path alone and came to a door and entered his house in the paddy fields just as his father dragged his reed bed out and burnt it, thinking his son had drowned in the rice. In those regions, death is not taken hard. A monsoon comes along, a tidal wave. The father clasped his son in his arms, the son stared over his shoulders. Mid-gaze — he was looking at the blue water, birds flying off and islands of reeds — the film ripped and a dull light brightened the cinema. 'The End!' the projectionist called from his cabin. 'Out!' A moth-eaten curtain, made of the same red plush the seats were covered in, fell down over the screen. I rose and went back outside with the other children.

No Lisette. I waited and waited. A cold wind drove scraps of paper and empty tins across a square where trees were growing in cement pots. I had on only my blue-and-white-striped vest and shorts and was freezing. Soon beat my arms against my body, then flapped round in circles like a duck and in the end — Lisette or no Lisette — flew up a broad street, Rämistrasse it was, that seemed like a continuation of the film to me, a hellish gorge, as I'd never seen so many cars, headlights flying past, well-lit trams and people everywhere. I flapped my wings in an attempt to dodge them. Incredible noise. I stood for a long time at Heimplatz, not daring to cross, to zip across between cars, then finally ran into the lights with my eyes shut and actually got to the other side. Behind me, tyres screeched and metal splintered. Hottingerstrasse was darker and calmer, apart from two ambulances and a police car with their wailing sirens and flashing blue lights racing past me when I got to the trees at the top. Soon, I was outside the house — my house nowadays — of which I knew not a thing, and yet my compass needle had been pointing to it the whole time. A tall, whitewashed house with lots of windows and black shutters. I shook the door, hammered a pane of glass behind which flowers were crowding and shouted, 'Hello! Hello!' as a light was on in the first floor. No response — nothing, no one — so I walked on a gravel strip round the house, to the back of it, where it was dark and the traffic sounded like sea waves crashing.

The moon bathed a fence, some flower boxes and the wall of the house in a blue light. The leaves of bushes and low trees rustled in the wind. A window was open, a hatch for cats, more like. I crawled through, ending up in a dark room in which only a slim beam of moonlight fell onto a desk, a typewriter and a tall pile of paper. I tore out the sheet in the typewriter and crumpled it up. On the floor above me, someone laughed. I didn't feel like laughing. On the contrary, I felt wretched and was still freezing. I curled up on the floor, my knees up to my chin, put my thumb in my mouth, clutched my fire engine with the other hand and fell asleep.

Hard to say how long I slept. Days perhaps. When I woke from the deepest of dreams — never before had I fallen into dreams so deeply — a warm sun was shining at any rate. But that wasn't what wakened me — the sun was protecting my sleep — but a strange feeling at my nose, a tickling, caused by a gigantic peacock feather trembling before my wide-open eyes and manoeuvred by the hand of a girl who was almost a young woman already. She looked at me, curious, and said, 'What are you doing here?'

'I'm waking up,' I mumbled.

'This is Papa's study,' the girl said. 'Even I am only allowed in when he gives me permission.'

'So?' I yawned and sat up. 'Has he given you permission?'

'He's not even at home.' She put the feather in her hair and now looked like an Indian. 'How did *you* get in?'

'Through the window.'

'And how come?'

She knelt beside me but was big in this position too. Already nearly like Lisette. She had brown hair and brown eyes behind her glasses with a black frame. Wore a top with a picture on it of men with their legs in different poses and guitars. And blue trousers.

'Who are they, on your vest?'

'My *vest*!' She screamed as if I'd said something completely mad. 'This is a T-shirt. XL, if you want to know. And these are New Kids on the Block. Are you still a baby, man?'

'I'm three,' I said. 'I'm hungry.'

'Now I know what you look like.' She pulled at my vest and shorts. 'Like an extraterrestrial. Do you eat earth food or do you want a cup of lubricating oil?'

'Lisette didn't come to get me. I feel I've not eaten for days.'

'It's okay,' she said a little sulkily. 'I was just joking.' She disappeared through a narrow door and clattered up a staircase. While she was pottering about upstairs, I looked around the room. Books on all the walls and strange pictures—the open stomach of a woman, for instance, with flowers growing from it. Two black statues stood on the floor, same as we had at home. This man had a penis with a red tip too and this woman also had a *v* between her legs. Newspapers lay everywhere. I took the pages beside the typewriter and threw them into the wastepaper basket. Stamped on them, to make space for them all. I'd just finished when the girl turned up again. She was walking carefully, like a tightrope walker, carrying a plate with something brown, something yellow and soft, from which steam rose. 'You'll be amazed. Secret recipe of mine.'

I bit into it. 'Delicious.'

'It's called Topping à la Mara. Cooking chocolate, melted cheese, sugar, mustard and croutons. I'm Mara.'

'Aha,' I said. 'I'm . . .'

'Man!' Mara exclaimed. 'You really remind me of someone. But *who is it*?'

She scrutinized me, pensively, seriously. I shrugged. She reminded me of no one. 'What did you say your name was?' But before I could open my mouth a second time, she screeched, 'Now I know!' dashed over to one of the bookshelves, returned with a book that was so big she had to carry it with both hands, a volume of photographs with a shabby grey cover. She sat down on the floor, leafed through it and eventually said, 'There!' She was pointing at a photo.

'That's me,' I said. 'That's our garden. The dog beside me is called Jimmy. And that one there is my Papa.'

'That's *my* Papa,' Mara said.

'Mine!'

'What I'm saying is,' Mara's voice became mellow, like that of a teacher explaining a problem to an especially obtuse pupil for the absolutely final time, 'the boy there is my Paps.'

'That would make you my daughter then,' I said and burst out laughing, panting and gasping till Mara hit me on the back.

'That photo's fifty years old,' she said. 'Man! You really are the spitting image of each other!'

I took the album from her and flipped further. She had a lot of photos of me! Of all of us! My father in his uniform among other soldiers, the only one with his helmet on. My mother looking out of the kitchen window, laughing, her mouth all sticky — she'd just had some bread and jam. I knew these pictures! Even Lisette, standing at the station — on the day she first came to us — in her travelling clothes and with a suitcase with cords round it. Then me again, in the branches of the Japanese tree, with a wry smile, as if I'd just bitten into one of its apples. Further back were other photos I didn't know. My mother at the top of a snowy mountain, wearing strange sunglasses that made her look blind. On a large-sized print, my father and beside him, a boy of about eight with an arm in plaster. Mara pointed to him. 'My Paps had broken his arm there. He fell from the apple tree. That one's my Grandad.'

'Hm,' I said, closing the album. Somehow, I was no longer interested in these photos. I licked the plate with Mara's topping clean and put it on the desk. Mara, watching me, suddenly screamed, 'Did you do that?' She pointed at the surface of the desk, now clear, and then at the wastepaper basket with all the crumpled paper.

I beamed at her and nodded.

'Man, man, man!' she groaned, pulling the sheets of paper from the basket. She smoothed out one after the other and put them back on the table. As she did so, she slapped her forehead and emitted high-pitched screams. 'Mad!' Eventually, she was pleased with her work and took two or three steps back, held her head at a slant and squinted her eyes. 'Maybe we'll get away with that.' She lifted the top sheet again, put it back carefully, bang on top of the one under it, nodded, suddenly took my hand and, via a hallway and a bathroom, whirled me back outside, back to the gravel strip on which a warm sun now shone and where we sat down on the empty flower boxes.

We were both panting. 'You're done for if I don't cover up for you. Just to let you know.'

'What? Who? How come?' I stuttered.

'If Paps notices that someone—his papers—my God! They're sacred. But I think I managed to put them back pretty well again.'

'Does he get so angry?'

'He'll rip your head off. Cross my heart. Want a cola chewing gum?'

I nodded. *I* had a nice Papa and was now trying to imagine one who rips heads off. Mara, meanwhile, had rummaged around in her pocket and found not only the chewing gum but also a photo, a crumpled passport photo of an old man with piercing eyes, a gigantic moustache and no hair. 'That's him—Paps.'

I put the gum in my mouth and looked at the man. He looked like a murderer, someone to fear. I bit into the gum and chewed.

'Well?' said Mara.

'Good,' I said, swallowing it.

'Do-o-o-n't!' she screamed, too late. 'I meant the photo. Of Paps.' She snatched it from me and put it back in her pocket. 'Have you never had chewing gum before?'

I shook my head. She tapped her forehead at me. The feather she still had in her hair shook, then fell down on the gravel. She looked at me as if I was a complete fool—I certainly felt like one—and went off. The garden gate was still open. I lifted the feather and ran it along the fence and the wall of the house for a while and when Mara still didn't come back, I went out to the street and the square with the trees, where I crouched behind the tree trunks, played hide-and-seek with the passers-by. If I couldn't see them, they couldn't see me either. Later, I stood for a long time at the window of a bakery, pressing my nose against it and, towards evening, I went back to the house.

Mara was, indeed, back in the garden. She was crouched in front of a hole in the wall of the house, the actual cat flap. I could now see the head of a cat in it, big eyes that were looking up at Mara. 'I'm just explaining to the cat,' she said, 'that I'm very fond of her though I'd really like to have a dog.'

'I need to go home,' I said. 'Here!' I held my red fire engine out to her. She took it and smiled. 'Thanks.' I shifted from one foot to the other,

wondering whether a kiss would be permissible,
but then, suddenly, she did it, took me by the
shoulders and turned me round and nudged me out
onto the street. Red and happy, I dashed off and
when I turned back again, at the square up ahead,
she was standing at the garden gate with the cat on
her arm, holding one of its paws and waving with
it. On the first floor, a window opened and a
woman leant out and called something. Mara's
mama, no doubt. She was blonde and I liked her,
quite unlike the father. I noticed only now that I
still had the peacock feather in my hand and ran,
as if my life was at stake, along Hottingerstrasse,
across Heimplatz and down Rämistrasse to the
cinema which I reached just as a woman was
beginning to bolt the doors. I rushed past her
sturdy legs into the dark hall that was full of people
again, adults, for this time I wasn't watching a
children's film but a story involving a war and dead
people. All I understood was that people can be
separated once and for all, with no possibility of
amends being made, separated for ever. At the end
of the film, of the life, the woman who at the

beginning had been young was now ancient and walking through the streets of a town she didn't know and her lover came towards her, all wrinkly now too, and they didn't recognize each other and simply walked on.

This time Lisette was there when I came out. She screamed when she saw me and clasped me in her arms. I wrapped her in my arms too and we both burst into tears. Then we took the same tram home — outside, it was still dark or dark once more and the tram had its windows covered — and, burbling excitedly, I told her how in the film the young man who did actually have a woman he loved, was grabbed by foreign soldiers and dragged far away to the dull steppes and I noticed only when we got off the tram that Lisette wasn't listening. She was staring ahead and biting her lips.

'What is it? What's wrong with you?'

'Nothing,' Lisette mumbled, starting to sob again. 'But how am I supposed to live without him?'

'But you have me,' I said.

Then, holding her hand, I walked in silence while she cried away to herself. The moon was also back and followed us. As we were passing the radio station, where the anti-aircraft gun was installed, I tickled her with the peacock feather until she sniffed, blew her nose, dried her eyes and smiled. 'For you,' I said, giving her the feather.

'How beautiful!' She admired it, really and truly, and caressed her cheeks with it. 'Where did you get it?'

'From Mara. She thinks I'm her father.'

'You have plenty of time for that still. Years, even,' Lisette said, laughing suddenly. 'You, a father!' I laughed too. Laughing, we toddled up the street that led to the house. Outside, the moon was shining on Mama, Papa and two men I didn't know. The two policemen. When they saw us, they screamed and all four came running towards us, waving and calling. The policemen were faster than my parents, much faster, and the fat one, who got to us first, lifted me, kissed me from head to toe and put me on his arm that was so big it reminded me of a tree trunk. He stank of tobacco. 'We've got the rascal!' he called back. 'We've got him!'

The lean policeman was humming round us like a spinning top and shouting over and over, 'Didn't we say we'd get him back? Didn't we promise?' His shadow was following him everywhere, black in the blue light.

'I'm hungry,' I said.

By now, my mother and father had also reached us and were trying to hug me and kiss me. The fat policeman wasn't letting go of me, though, and began to dance, like a hippo, roaring and bawling, and so they danced too, in order to be close to me, and soon the whole bunch was dancing, the boss, his assistant, Mama, Papa and Lisette. I was being swung above them and squealing. We danced into the house and up the stairs, into the flat, where the policeman kept me on his knee and bounced me up and down, bumpety-bump, while my mother made spaghetti in the kitchen. My father had turned on the gramophone, a trunk-sized monster that was now playing very loud, triumphal music with a lot of trumpets. He sang to it, the small

policeman squawked along and suddenly the fat
policeman too joined in, singing so close to me I
got a fright and put my hands up to my ears.
Lisette stood the whole time, lost in thought, at
the window, looking out into the night. Then the
spaghetti arrived. They all watched me, as if an
eating child was something special. When I was
finished, I pushed my plate away and said, 'Topping
à la Mara is much better.'

'What's better?' my mother said.

'Jimmy,' Lisette said, as if she'd just become
aware of something really decisive. 'Where's
Jimmy?'

The small policeman jumped up. 'Leave him to
us. We'll get him back. Won't we, Kuno?'

The fat policeman nodded. 'He's right there,
Frieder. We'll get him back too. But now we have
to go.' He snapped to attention, saluted as if he were
wearing a uniform and the two of them marched
out. The door clicked shut behind them and we sat
there, quiet now, for half the night.

New days, other years, came along. I got
bigger, fell out of the apple tree and had my arm in

plaster. The war had gone away, peace had come. The soda siphon stood, remained, on top of the cabinet. No one ever squirted from it again. I often looked up at it when sunlight was sparkling in the blue glass. Then I'd stand in the garden and hope Jimmy might come up the path, suddenly, nuzzling the ground as he did. But he didn't come back. He'd vanished. The sun shone, the meadows shone. Now, though, I reckoned a sudden bang could tear everything apart. NOW. I looked up to the sky, into the blue. Were I to see a black dot, I wouldn't have much time any more. Maybe my silhouette would be etched on the wall of the house. My father would have vanished. My mother would have vanished. Lisette would have vanished. They wouldn't exist any more. They don't exist any more — Father, Mother, Lisette, and not Jimmy either, the dog.